CHUCK
and
WOODCHUCK

Cece Bell

Candlewick Press

MY NAME IS CAROLINE, and I am in the first grade.

One day at school, we had show-and-tell.
I brought my grandfather's ukulele from Hawaii.
I told the other kids everything I knew about it
(except how to play it—I sure didn't know how).

Everyone else had neat stuff to show, too —

including Chuck. He brought a woodchuck.
And all Chuck said was "This is Woodchuck."

Woodchuck just smiled at us. And then . . .

Woodchuck started playing with some of our show-and-tell stuff! It was hilarious!

Woodchuck was so cute and funny that even
our teacher agreed that he should come
to school every day. So that is what he did.

Woodchuck was friendly with everyone at school . . .

but he was especially sweet to me.

Once, when my ears got cold while we were playing outside . . .

Woodchuck gave me a hat to wear.

I think it was Chuck's hat.
I was grateful.

I tried to return it when we went back inside.
But Chuck just turned red and shook his head.

Another time, when I accidentally dropped my cupcake
on the floor during our Halloween party . . .

Woodchuck came over and
gave me a whole new cupcake.

I think it was Chuck's!

I laughed and tried to give it back,
but Chuck pushed it back into my hands.

In the spring, when I messed up my
April flowers painting in art class . . .

Woodchuck brought over the painting that
Chuck had made and gave it to me.

It was beautiful.

I waved at Chuck to thank him.
I think he waved back.

Chuck!

I wanted to thank him backstage, but we were supposed to be super quiet during the play.

So I smiled at him instead.
He actually smiled back!

A few days later, our school pictures arrived.
Woodchuck took one of mine . . .

and gave it to Chuck!
I am sure I saw Woodchuck wink at me.

Chuck didn't wink, though. Believe it or not, he spoke!
To me!

Of course I said yes.
So we all walked home together.

For the kids at the Blacksburg New School

First edition 2016

Library of Congress Catalog Card Number 2015933239
ISBN 978-0-7636-7524-0

15 16 17 18 19 20 TWP 10 9 8 7 6 5 4 3 2 1

Printed in Johor Bahru, Malaysia

This book was typeset in Kosmik.
The illustrations were done in ink and colored digitally.

Candlewick Press
99 Dover Street
Somerville, Massachusetts 02144

visit us at www.candlewick.com